The Sleepover Club

Have you been
invited to all these
sleepovers?

Sleepover Girls Go Snowboarding

by Sue Mongredien

Collins

An Imprint of HarperCollinsPublishers

The Sleepover Club ® is a
registered trademark of HarperCollins*Publishers* Ltd

First published in Great Britain by Collins in 1999
Collins is an imprint of HarperCollins*Publishers* Ltd
77-85 Fulham Palace Road, Hammersmith,
London, W6 8JB

The HarperCollins website address is
www.**fire**and**water**.com

1 3 5 7 9 8 6 4 2

Text copyright © Sue Mongredien 1999

Original series characters, plotlines
and settings © Rose Impey 1997

ISBN 0 00675450-3

The author asserts the moral right to
be identified as the author of the work.

Printed and bound in Great Britain by
Caledonian International Book Manufacturing Ltd,
Glasgow G64

Sleepover Kit List

1. Sleeping bag
2. Pillow
3. Pyjamas or a nightdress
4. Slippers
5. Toothbrush, toothpaste, soap etc
6. Towel
7. Teddy
8. A creepy story
9. Food for a midnight feast:
    chocolate, crisps, sweets, biscuits.
    In fact anything you like to eat.
10. Torch
11. Hairbrush
12. Hair things like a bobble or hairband,
    if you need them
13. Clean knickers and socks
14. Change of clothes for the next day
15. Sleepover diary and membership card

CHAPTER ONE

Yo! How's it going?

It's Kenny here if you hadn't guessed – yep, I'm back, fans! Well, let's face it, there was no way I was letting any of the others tell you this story. I mean, puh-leeeze, it was all down to me that we went snowboarding in the first place...

Oops – getting ahead of myself as usual. My mum reckons I'm always doing that – charging off without warning. Maybe I'm just a bit too impatient to do everything properly all the time. So what, though! That's just me – the original Action Girl – I like everything to happen fast! Hanging around is for wallpaper, that's what I say...

So where was I? Oh yes. Snowboarding. Have you ever tried it? It is AWESOME!!!! It's the most exciting, dangerous, scary, fun thing I can think of – well, except our sleepovers, of course... Mind you, not that I'll be able to go on the slopes again for a while, 'cos— oops, I'll have to tell you that later. Better not ruin the story on the first page, eh!

I like all sports really – especially football. And gymnastics. And I'm mad about swimming. And running. You get the idea. But snowboarding is something else altogether! As soon as I'm a rich and famous surgeon, I'm going to splash out on a no-expense-spared snowboarding holiday for the Sleepover Club, off in Colorado or somewhere – Nick says there are some WICKED slopes there.

Now I know you'll be confused. Who's Nick, then? you're thinking. And you might even be thinking, who are the Sleepover Club when they're at home?! Don't worry – I'm about to explain everything!

There's five of us in the Sleepover Club – me and Frankie, who are best mates, plus Fliss, Lyndz and Rosie. As a quick intro to the others, I'll do this thing Mrs Weaver got us to do the other day at school.

OK, say the five of us were all different types of... I don't know... bag. So I'd be a sports bag, right? That one's easy. Frankie would be a sparkly, space-age kind of bag with cool gadgets and inventions all over it – she loves that sort of thing. Some people at school think Frankie is pretty weird because she comes out with these off-the-wall ideas all the time, but she's just an original, which is a good thing if you ask me. You'll recognise Frankie when you see her – she's really tall and she'll probably be wearing something freaky as usual.

Who next? Well, Fliss is another easy one. If Fliss was a bag, she would be a pink and fluffy girly kind of handbag with a lace trim and frills all over it. Yuck!!! Just the sort of thing I hate. Oh, and it would be a designer model too, of course – and very expensive. Fliss is big on things like that. She loves clothes, make-up, jewellery, doing people's hair and the colour pink. Say no more! I suppose she's quite pretty if you like that sort of thing – but there's being pretty, and then there's being pretty and really boring about it. Unfortunately, our Fliss is more like the second of the two...

That's enough of me being horrible. Lyndz next – let's see. Lyndz's bag would probably have pictures of animals all over it – especially pictures of horses and dogs. Oh, and when you bought it, some of the proceeds would go to a kittens' orphanage or a sanctuary for retired donkeys. Yes, Lyndz is truly nuts about animals – she'd do anything for them. Lyndz is kind of soppy sometimes too, but only in a nice way. She also gets the loudest hiccups you've ever heard in your life. Scary!!

Last but not least, Rosie. I've left her till last because she only joined our school fairly recently. Surprise surprise, Lyndz felt sorry for her 'cos she didn't know anyone, and invited her to join our club. The rest of us were a bit mad at first because we don't let just anyone join – but it turned out to be a good thing as

Rosie is brilliant fun. The best thing about Rosie is her sense of humour though, so I reckon her bag would be quite trendy and nice, and would have something that made you laugh on it.

Anyway, the five of us are all in the same class at school, and we do just about everything together out of school too. Best of all, every weekend we have a sleepover at someone's house. And guess what? That's why we're called the Sleepover Club! DERRRR!

Ever been to a sleepover? They are just the coolest thing. We all take our night stuff and torches and Sleepover diaries, and everyone brings loads of sweets that we can munch through the night. We play loads of ace games and then stay up all night telling horror stories or jokes. Sleepovers are the best!!

I tell a pretty mean horror story if I say so myself – Fliss gets scared sometimes and says she feels sick (what a wuss!!) while the rest of us get all giggly and screechy. You know when just the slightest thing gets you all scared and hysterical, and your heart starts beating dead fast, and then someone makes you JUMP?! Like that. <u>EEEEEEK!!</u>

Like the other week, when we were sleeping over at Lyndz's, I told the others this story I'd got from my dad (he's a doctor, so he tells me all the goriest, grossest things!!). He told me that in the olden days, about five hundred years ago, the doctors used to cure people by sticking leeches on them – 'cos they thought that while the leeches were sucking out your blood, they'd suck out all the bad stuff in you that was making you ill as well! Is that just gross or what?! YUCK!!

You know what's it like if you're lying there in the dark and getting all scared about something, though. Anything sets you off! Everyone was groaning and making "ugh" noises at my leech story – and of course Fliss was saying she felt sick as usual – so I decided to play a trick on Frankie, who I was lying next to.

"Imagine all those leeches on your body slurping away at your blood," I said in a deep spooky voice, "and imagine them slithering over you to get to another juicy bit!" And then I made this huge slurpy noise and scrabbled my fingers through Frankie's hair.

"*Aaaaaargh!!!*"

She let out this ginormous scream and I collapsed in giggles. Frankie can be mega LOUD sometimes! All the others jumped – but then when they heard me laughing, they all cracked up too.

Frankie whacked me round the head with a pillow. "Cow!" she yelled at me.

"Leech-brain!" I yelled back, whacking her so hard I toppled over and landed on her.

Somehow we had totally forgotten it was the middle of the night and we were meant to be quiet. Soon all five of us were having this free-for-all pillow fight in the dark. Ever done that? It is so funny! You don't know where anyone is, and you're just whacking away, hoping to get someone – and now and then you hear a scream and know you've hit a target!

Suddenly – *crash!* The door was flung open and there was Lyndz's dad standing in the doorway.

"It's a giant leech!" Lyndz yelled and we all screamed hysterically.

Lyndz's dad switched the light on and blinked at the mess everywhere. Pillows thrown all over the place, sleeping bags tangled up where we'd scrambled out of them – and the five of us all out of breath and looking a bit spooked! Lyndz's dad is a teacher at the comprehensive, so he's a pro at telling kids off if he's narked. He was a bit cross 'cos we'd woken baby Sam up. Uh-oh...

So sometimes my horror stories get us into trouble – but most of the time we can get away with it!

Anyway, back to this story. Ready? Tell you what – why don't we go and sit in my garden while I tell you the whole lot? We can swing on the swings while I'm telling you – and then we can do some of those flying swing jumps off when we get really high. Come on – this way. Then I'll tell you EVERYTHING!

CHAPTER TWO

Right. Story. Well, I suppose it started on a Saturday. It was the beginning of November, and of course Fliss the Virgo wanted us all to go Christmas shopping. No offence if you're a Virgo or anything, but they're just a bit too organised for me. You should see Fliss's bedroom – everything's arranged in neat little piles or hidden away in storage units, and everything matches. Pink. Very pink. Personally, my "storage unit" is the space under my bed, where I stuff everything. At least that way if I lose something, I'm pretty sure where it will be.

But anyway, Felicity "Miss Organised 1999" Sidebotham wanted us to go Christmas shopping, even though Christmas was absolutely weeks and weeks away. Christmas shopping's for Christmas Eve, that's what I say, but sometimes you just can't argue with Fliss. She gets that stubborn look on her face, and you know that's it! You've got to go along with her.

Rosie talked me into it in the end. "I'm not going to be buying anything either, 'cos I'm skint," she said, frank as ever. "But we could go Christmas *wish*-shopping – where we look for things we want as presents from other people!"

Ooh! I liked the sound of that much more. "Brilliant one, Rosie," I said. "The new sports shop it is, then!"

The others all groaned. "Ooh, surprise us," said Frankie, rolling her eyes. "Let me guess... Could it possibly be something to do with..."

"Football!" everyone yelled out together.

I grinned. Did I mention that I love football?!

Ahh. I already told you.

"C'mooooon you Foxes!" I shouted, jumping up and down. "I want to have a look at the new strip – I mean, we're three months into the season and I haven't even got the new top yet!"

Us five always have a good laugh in town – even if Fliss does drag us round every single clothes shop most of the time. YAWWWWWN! First of all, we went into Boots because Lyndz wanted to get some bubble bath for her mum. Fliss spent ages examining every type of nail varnish while we were in there, leaving me, Frankie and Rosie in front of this shelf of all sorts of yucky things like wart cream and sprays for smelly feet.

"OK, who can find the grossest thing?" Rosie said. "We should club together and buy it for someone we don't like."

"How about these drops for hard ear wax?" Frankie suggested. "That's pretty gross."

"Here's some athlete's foot powder," I said, and started reading from the label. "*For flaky, itchy feet.* Yuck!! No thanks!"

"What about this spray for bad breath?" Rosie giggled. "Ugh! Just imagine how embarrassing it would be, buying that!"

Lyndz came up just then. "What are you lot all sniggering about?" she asked. "Fliss wants us to help her choose some perfume – she's going to ask her mum for some for Christmas."

I couldn't help groaning. "Poo, you won't catch me wearing any stinky perfume," I said, as we started walking to the perfume counter. "It all smells horrible!"

"What – even this one?" Frankie said – then grabbed a tester bottle and sprayed this yucky sickly perfume all over me.

"Aaaargh!" I shouted, coughing and choking. It really was *foul*! "Right, Frankie Thomas," I said, "you've asked for it now!" And I grabbed another tester bottle and squirted her with it. "Now you stink too!"

Fliss was so embarrassed, she dragged us out of the shop. As we all walked along the street, people kept giving us funny looks. We really did pong!!

Then I stopped dead on the pavement. "My

turn!" I said. "We're going in here next."

The others groaned as I led them into the new Mega Sports shop that had just opened in Cuddington. I'd been badgering my mum and dad all week to take me into town to check it out – and at last I was going to get to see it.

Woweee! It was a wicked shop. Heaven! I wanted to move in! Loads and loads of footy stuff, which of course I checked out straightaway. Loads of nice trackie tops and trainers – definitely a few to put on the Christmas wish-list there...

And then I found this whole surf and ski section at the back of the shop, which was just *awesome*. Lots of boards and all the gear – and there were these three tellies on the wall showing snowboarding videos. The sight of the snowboarders skimming down impossible slopes, doing jumps and turns, just made my legs go wobbly with excitement. It looked f-f-fantastic!!

"Hey, Frankie, check this out!" I shouted, waving some snow goggles in the air. "Snowboarding!"

I think I must have shouted quite loudly – me? Loud? Impossible! – because suddenly this guy appeared next to me.

"Ahh, a snowboarding fan!" he said. He sounded like someone off *Neighbours* so I guessed he had to be an Aussie.

"I wish," I said to him. "I've never tried it, but it looks wicked."

"Oh, it's the best," he said, enthusiastically. "It is so cool! You go so fast, the world's like a blur – and then once you get in the half-pipe, you can really start having some serious fun."

"Wow," I breathed. I wasn't quite sure what he was on about, but it sounded good.

"Yeah, it is pretty wow!" he laughed. "You should try it – get out on those slopes. It's the most exciting thing you can get into. Believe me, I'm an addict!"

"Mega!" I said, just as Frankie wandered over.

"Well, it's quite easy to pick up," he said. "You should give it a go. All you need is good balance, good co-ordination – and nerves of steel!"

"And snow," I pointed out.

"Snow helps," he agreed. "Fingers crossed we get some soon, eh?"

"Fingers crossed," I said fervently, crossing as many as I could.

"Well, if you ever want any advice or tips about snowboarding, just come and have a chat with me any time," he said, smiling. "The name's Nick."

"Kenny," I said, suddenly feeling shy as we shook hands. "Thanks."

Nick suddenly coughed and wrinkled his nose. "Can you smell something?" he said. "I think the cleaner's gone a bit mad with the air freshener this week!"

I could hardly keep a straight face as he went off to serve someone. As soon as he was out of earshot, Frankie elbowed me and we collapsed in giggles.

"Air freshener!" I snorted. "I knew that perfume smelled horrible!"

"Maybe Fliss should just ask for a can of that for Christmas instead!" Frankie giggled. "Save her mum a bit of dosh, anyway!"

21

Once we'd pulled ourselves together, I noticed the others had left the shop and were waiting outside for us. "We'd better go, I suppose..." I said reluctantly.

"Found the footy top you want, then?" Frankie asked.

"I think I've found something better," I told her, pointing up at one of the videos where someone was going a 90-degree turn in mid-air, like it was the easiest thing in the world. "Snowboarding," I said. "That's what I want!"

You know what I'm like. Once I get one of my brilliant ideas in my head, it's impossible for me to think about other stuff. Suddenly I really really *really* wanted to go snowboarding, more than anything else in the world!

I could just imagine myself whizzing down those slopes, a spray of snow flying up behind me, hat and sun-goggles on, arms out to keep my balance... WOW!! What a thought!

Lyndz had something else on her mind, though.

"Lunch time!" she said loudly as soon as we

got out of the shop. "I'm STARVING!"

"Lyndz, you're always starving," Fliss said disapprovingly. Fliss's mum thinks we should all live off carrot sticks and sunflower seeds – and sometimes I think Fliss agrees with her. Fliss even went on a diet once – I mean, D-U-M-B or what?!

"Maybe you've got worms, Lyndz," I said to wind her up. "Dad says they make you feel hungry all the time."

"*Eeeeugh!*" Rosie said, pretending to be sick. "Gross, Kenny!"

"I have not got worms!" Lyndz said hotly. "I just feel like a cheeseburger, that's all."

"Yeah, you look a bit like one, too," I said, dodging out of her way as she tried to whack me with her bag.

"You're in a good mood for someone who hates shopping," Fliss said suspiciously. "What's got into you?"

"I wish a cheeseburger would get into me," Lyndz was moaning. "Like, now."

"I'm on a mission, that's what," I said mysteriously.

"What, with that bloke in the shop?" Frankie said, winking at me. "They looked very cosy when I walked over there!"

"Get knotted!" I said crossly, but they'd all creased up giggling and Lyndz started making smoochy kissing noises in my ear.

"He was quite a babe actually, wasn't he?" Fliss said thoughtfully. "Not as nice as Ryan Scott, though."

"Well, now we know what Kenny's type is like," Lyndz said between giggles. "Action Man! What a perfect couple you two would make! *Mwaaah!!*"

"Shut up!" I said.

"Ooh, getting a bit hot and bothered, are we?" Rosie teased, elbowing me. "You must like him!"

"I don't like him – well, he was OK, I suppose," I said. For some reason I was blushing like anything. "It's snowboarding I'm into now! That's my mission!"

"Oh, here we go," Fliss sighed. "I thought it was trampolining you wanted us all to get into?"

"That was last week," I said. "But this sounds much more fun! Even better – it sounds much more *dangerous!* You have to have nerves of steel to try it, Nick said!"

Fliss did this big dramatic groan like she'd rather eat worms. As I told you, she's a bit of a wuss sometimes, especially when it comes to my brilliant ideas. Nerves of steel? Nerves of cotton wool, more like!

In fact, me and Fliss are pretty different in a lot of ways. When we have a sleepover at hers, she always tries to get us to play hairdressers and girly stuff like that – and sometimes she won't join in my ideas for games because she thinks they're "too rough" or she doesn't want to mess her hair up. Honestly! The only time I ever even think about my hair is when Mum is brushing out the tangles and I'm yelling with pain. Some people are weird, aren't they?

"This way," Lyndz said, shepherding us into the burger joint. "Unless you want me passing out from hunger, that is?"

I started telling them all about the things I'd seen on the snowboarding videos in the shop while we were queuing up to get some lunch.

"And then I saw this one bloke doing a jump like this, right," I said, whizzing round quickly in the queue just like the guy on the video.

Uh-oh. Bad idea…

"Whoops!"

"Oh, look where you're going, young lady!"

I'd just sent someone's vanilla milkshake flying! It shot through the air and splattered all over the floor, spraying our feet with sticky white goo.

I bit my lip. Things like that are always happening to me – I don't know why.

"Sorry," I said to this lady who was looking furiously at me, and I scrabbled in my purse. "I'll get you another one."

"I should think so too!" she snorted. Stuck-up prune. Didn't she know a snowboarder in the making when she saw one?

We finally got to sit down with our lunches and the others all started teasing me again about Nick. Rosie started doing her terrible Aussie accent, every time she said anything.

"I bet he likes hanging out in Summer Bay,"

she drawled. "Awww, surf's up – chuck another shrimp on the barbie, willya?"

"You sound like Rolf Harris – go back to *Animal Hospital*, will you?" I growled. "And get yourself a brain operation while you're there!"

"Ahh, fair dinkum, Sheila!" Frankie giggled.

"Tie me kangaroo down, sport!" Lyndz added, laughing so hard that milkshake shot straight out of her nose – both sides!!

"*Eeeeurggghhh!*" squealed Fliss, turning away hurriedly.

"Gross!" Frankie said, sticking her tongue out and laughing at the same time.

"Yeee-uck!" Rosie wailed.

"Can you tell what it is yet?" I yelled, doing my own Rolf impression.

By now we were all laughing hysterically, and were creased up over the tables. For a minute I even forgot all about the idea of going snowboarding. Not for very long, though...

CHAPTER THREE

Well, the next thing that happened was that I went home and found out that my parents had been abducted by aliens – and even better, the aliens had taken my gross sisters too!

Nah, not really. Just checking to see if you're paying attention, or if you're skimming through to get to the best bits. Sneaky, eh? Mind you, I'm the biggest skimmer in our class. Sometimes you just want to skip ahead to see what's going to happen at the end, don't you? I can't stand waiting!

Anyway, no aliens in this story unfortunately. No, the next thing that really happened was that after being dragged around a few boring clothes shops by Fliss, we all went back to our own homes.

Saturday tea-time means chips and everything in our house. YUM! My favourite tea – I'm a champion chip-eater. Even better, Emma (oldest sister – OK but a bit bossy) is going through this teenage "Don't want to get fat, don't want to get spots" phase at the moment so she isn't touching anything remotely greasy. You know what that means, don't you? All the more for ME! I've got her so sussed that if she even looks at a chip, all I have to do is say, "Terrible for your skin, Em," and she'll back away as if it's going to infect her with the plague, just by sitting there on a plate. Fantastic!

Of course, Molly (other sister – and horrible pig I have to share a bedroom with) still shovels them down her neck like the Cuddington Potato Famine has broken out, worse luck. And she wonders why I call her

Molly the Monster... Plus, she's skinny as anything and hasn't got a spot near her, so I can't use my Emma tactics on her. YET!

Anyway, I decided I might as well start on the Kenny-Goes-Snowboarding campaign straight away.

"Mum, you know for Christmas this year..." I started saying through a mouthful of sausage and tomato ketchup.

Mum raised her eyebrows. "Yes..." she said.

"I sense our daughter is about to put in a request for something," Dad said, clapping a hand to his forehead. "I just get that feeling..."

I ignored him. "Well, you know we always go to Grandma's, or Granny Mack's for Christmas?"

"Yes..." Mum said in a suspicious what-does-Kenny-want-this-time? kind of voice.

"Spit it out, love," Dad said.

"Well, what do you think about going abroad this year? Going on holiday? Maybe somewhere snowy," I said, crossing my fingers under the table so tightly I nearly cut my blood supply off.

"Laura, what are you getting at?" Mum said. "What's all this about?"

"I just thought it would be nice to do something different," I said casually, shrugging as if I hadn't really thought about it. (Yeah, *right!*)

"She wants to go snowboarding, Mum," Molly the Monster said smugly. "I heard her talking to Frankie about it on the phone."

"Shut up!" I said crossly, kicking her. "Mind your own business!"

"What's snowboarding?" Mum asked, looking puzzled.

"It's like skateboarding but without snow," Dad said. "Kind of." He didn't look very impressed. "Andrew McCarthy broke his leg doing it – he's still on crutches because of it."

"Oh, it's not dangerous," I said breezily. "You could always go skiing if you didn't want to snowboard."

"I don't know why we're even having this conversation," Mum said, putting her knife and fork down. "What makes you think we can afford a holiday at the moment anyway? Because I'll tell you now – we can't."

"PLEEEEEASE," I said, going down on my hands and knees in front of them and making my eyes go as puppy-dog as they could. "Please, please, please – you don't have to buy me a Christmas present or anything if you say we can go!"

"Who said you were getting anything anyway?" my dad said – joking, I hope.

"Oh, go on, Mum," I said, trying to ignore my dad. "You'd say yes if you luuurrrved me..."

"I'm saying no *because* we love you – because we don't want our little girl to break her leg!" Mum said. "Now eat your tea before it gets cold."

I scowled. Little girl – ugh!! Sometimes I can't wait to be old. It's so unfair that parents get to decide everything all the time.

"Don't cry, little girl," Molly said sarcastically, pulling a horrible face at me. "Ahhh, diddums!"

I whacked her one. "You'll be crying in a minute," I warned her.

"Girls, if you keep fighting, we won't be going anywhere – not even to Grandma's," Dad warned.

I sulked and stabbed a chip, wishing it was Molly I was plunging a fork into. GRRR! Sometimes she is just...

"How about one of those indoor places?" Emma said suddenly. "Maybe you could go there for a day instead – there's meant to be one around here somewhere."

"Not the same," I growled, through a mouthful of chip, too cross with my mean parents to be interested.

"Suit yourself," she said, shrugging. "*Little* sister."

I had a moan about it to the others at school on Monday.

"I can't believe they won't even think about taking us on holiday," I said mournfully. "Why do parents have to be so boring?"

"I'd rather go and lie on a beach for my holiday," Fliss said, wrinkling her nose up. "I agree with them – I wouldn't want to go, either.

33

All that cold snow, ugh! You wouldn't get much of a tan."

"Christmas would be weird in another country anyway," said Lyndz. "I like being at home with everyone around. Waking up in my own bed on Christmas morning, you know."

"And it would cost a bomb, all of you going away," Rosie pointed out.

"I can't exactly imagine your dad snowboarding either," Frankie said, with a laugh. "His glasses would come flying off and he'd crash straight into something!"

"But *I'd* love it," I said, wistfully. "I'd really, really love it. There must be a way round it somehow..."

"Oh, no," Rosie teased. "Kenny's got her thinking head on – and you know what that means!"

"She'll be building her own snow mountain in the village!" Lyndz said, giggling.

"And pushing Molly down head-first," Frankie said. "I'll help you, Kenz!"

I sniffed. No-one was taking this very seriously! "You may scoff," I said grandly. "But you wait – I'll get my snow one way or another!"

On my way home that night, I got thinking. If *they* weren't bothered, *I* was! What could I do?

As I was kicking my shoes off in the hall, I spotted Emma's skateboard. Aha! Snowboard, skateboard – well, it would be a start, anyway. Now all I needed was some snow – and a slope!

Well, snow was out of the question; it had been as clear as anything all day with no sign of any snow-clouds. Hmmm.

And then I had another brilliant idea. The stairs!

I stood at the top with the skateboard and took a deep breath. Well, here goes! I said to myself. I got on the board and pushed myself off and...

WOOOOAAAHHHHH!! I hurtled down the stairs, bump, bump, bump – crack. OUCH!

Results – one cracked head.

One furious sister.

One cross mum saying it was my own fault.

One mad dad saying stairboarding was banned for life in his house.

I'm telling you – don't bother. Far too much aggro for about five seconds of excitement!

The only thing to do was to go back to Mega Sports to get some advice from Nick. He was the one person who could help me in my hour of need – and this time, I'd make sure I didn't stink the shop out, either!

Next day at school, as soon as Mrs Weaver said it was home time, I charged out of the classroom like Roadrunner with ants in his pants. ACTION!

The others cornered me as I was taking off my bike lock in the staff car park. The five of us usually hang around together after school a bit, waiting for our mums to pick us up – or we walk or cycle part of the way back home together.

"What's the big hurry, Kenz?" Frankie asked curiously.

"Mum says I can go to Mega Sports before I go home today," I said, strapping my helmet on. "I want to talk to that Nick bloke again."

"Oh, yeah," Rosie said, all sarcastic. "I see. We see, don't we, girls?"

"Kenny, you're going all red," Fliss said smugly. "Over a boy!"

"He's not a boy, he's a man," I said. Bad thing to say, Kenny! As soon as the words were out of my mouth, they all started giggling.

"Ooh, he's a real man!" Lyndz said, laughing so hard that she was holding her tummy and bending over.

"Shut UP!" I yelled, getting on my bike quickly. I couldn't stand much more of this!

"Well, now you've got a boyfriend, don't forget about your friends – us," Frankie said, sounding a bit put out.

"He is not my boyfriend!" I shouted. "For the last time..."

"Ooh, has Laura got a boyfriend?" someone cooed in a sickly kind of voice. "Who would go out with her? He must be blind!"

"Or mad!" another voice simpered.

Oh, great. That was all I needed. We'd made so much noise, the M&Ms had heard us!

(If you don't know – the M&Ms are Emma Hughes and Emily Berryman. They're our sworn enemies and just totally vile girls that should be put down for the good of the human race. But you'll see that for yourself, before too long anyway.)

"Don't call me Laura," I said through gritted teeth, as they walked over, giggling stupidly. "And get out of my way before I run you over!"

"Oh, I am scared," said Emily, or Goblin-features as we sometimes call her. "Look, Em, I'm just shaking in fear of Laura."

"Right, you asked for it, Berryman!" I said, and charged my bike straight for her. She squealed and dodged out of the way just before I got to her. Rats!

"I'll get my brother on to you if you lay a finger on me!" she yelled after me, sounding a bit shocked.

"Ooh, puh-leeeze don't scare me!" I shouted back, grinning to myself. "Bye, you lot!" I called out to the others. And with that, I shot off, pedalling as fast as I could.

CHAPTER FOUR

I love sports shops. I must have been in a million of them and it's like being in Kenny paradise, surrounded by all the football stuff and tennis racquets and swimming costumes. Every time I go in I have this stupid fantasy where I'm a millionaire, come to spend, spend, spend – and I end up buying the whole shop!

I walked around slowly, and then I saw Nick again, sorting out a box of sunglasses at the far end of the shop, just near the surf and ski section. Aha!

He looked up and smiled as I walked over.

"Hello again," he said. "Kelly, wasn't it?"

I blushed horribly. Oh, no! Blushing! I was turning into a right girl!

"Kenny," I said. "It's a nickname."

"Oh – sorry, Kenny," he said. "What are you up to, then? Come back for another look at this snow gear?"

"Yeah," I said. "I haven't been able to stop thinking about it."

He shook his head, eyes twinkling. "Oh, mate," he said. "You've got it bad, haven't you? You're as bad as me! Only problem is, there's no snow, right?"

"I've been practising on my sister's skateboard, but it's not really the same," I confessed.

"It's not a bad idea, though," he said. "It'll help you practise keeping your balance, I suppose." He looked thoughtful. "Want to have a go on a real board? Just standing, I mean?"

I nodded, feeling all shy again. For some reason, I couldn't think of anything to say. Yeah – I know what you're thinking. Me, motormouth, lost for words! I'd never had that feeling before.

He got a turquoise-coloured board down from the rack and put it on the shop floor. It looked massive!

"Are they all that big?" I asked, my eyes popping.

He grinned at me. "There are junior sizes too, but we've only got the adult ones in the shop at the moment," he said. "Take your shoes off, anyway. What size foot are you?"

"Three," I said, hoping it didn't sound too babyish. I unlaced my school shoes and stood there in my socks.

"Try a pair of these on," he said, passing me a pair of black boots.

I could hardly tie up the laces, my fingers had suddenly gone so trembly. "There," I said finally. "Blimey, they're heavy, aren't they?"

"Need to be, mate," he said. "You need good, solid support round your ankles when you're 'boarding. Don't want you toppling over to the side, do we?"

"Suppose not," I said. I'm telling you, my feet

really did look cool in those boots. I suddenly wished the others were there to see me, Kenny, about to have a go on a real, humungously big snowboard!

"Now, step on to the board," he told me. "Let me fix the bindings for you." He fastened up some straps and clasps – and then suddenly my feet were firmly joined to the board. It felt dead weird!

I tried lifting a foot up experimentally – and nothing happened, except I gave this sort of wobble...

"Whoooaaaa!" I said, arms flailing about.

Nick grabbed hold of me. "Easy, tiger," he said, laughing at my face. "Not as easy as it looks, is it, just standing still?"

"It's so weird!" I said. "And you can really slide down snowy mountains on one of these?"

"Oh, yeah!" he said, chuckling. "And it's a lot more exciting than just standing in a sports shop in Cuddington, I can tell you! To take a corner, you just have to lean to the left or right – and round you go!"

I closed my eyes and put my arms out to the sides to keep my balance. "OK, I'm in the Swiss Alps," I said, imagining as hard as I could. "It's a gorgeous sunny day and there's tons of snow everywhere."

"And you're right at the top of this awesome mountain and... you're off!" Nick said, going along with my pretend. "And you're whizzing down as fast as you can go, snow spraying up on either side of you – to the left, to the right – watch out for that tree!"

I opened my eyes with a jump, and we both started to laugh.

"You're pretty good for a beginner," he teased. "Shame about the tree, though!"

"Oh, well, it shouldn't have been in my way," I joked. I looked down at my feet and sighed. "I wish Leicester wasn't quite so... flat," I said.

"Not many mountains around, are there?" Nick agreed.

"I'm trying to talk my mum and dad into a snowy holiday over Christmas," I said hopefully – even though I knew it was about as likely as them taking us to Mars after my stairboarding tricks. "Where would be a good place to go?"

His eyes brightened at the thought. "Well, at this time of year, France would be good enough, if you don't want to go far. The Alps would be great – there are some wicked resorts there. Or Italy. Or Switzerland. Or Austria. And we Aussies get snow too, in Victoria..."

He groaned out loud, then laughed as he started unfastening my boots. "Now we're just torturing ourselves," he said. "There's always those indoor places if you can't talk your parents into a holiday."

I frowned. "It's not really the same though, is it?"

He shook his head. "It's not the same, but it's better than nothing." He yanked the boots off my feet and put them back in a box. "At least you can learn how to do it before you get on the real slopes, eh?"

"True," I said, thoughtfully. I'd just remembered Emma saying something about it the other night, only I'd been too cross to pay any attention. Hmmm!

"Well, pop in any time you want more info – always happy to help out a fellow fan," he said. "I can bore you with more of my stories about surfing and snowboarding my way around the world for as long as you like!"

"Thanks!" I blurted out, feeling myself going pink. "Brilliant!" (I know it sounds like I'm being Flissy but he really did have a nice smile. Honest!)

"No probs, Kenny," he said. "See you around!"

I cycled home as if I was cycling on air. As you know, I'm not the soppy type AT ALL, but Nick was really... *amazing*. The kind of person I just wanted to talk to for hours and hours and hours. He was so COOL – to think he'd been to all those places and could do all those excellent, exciting, dangerous things! I was just totally *totally* impressed, and suddenly understood what Mrs Weaver was on about when she talked about role models. I'd never really paid much attention to it before, but now I had my very own role model – I wanted to be just like Nick!

* * *

After school the next day, I went round to Frankie's house for tea before Brownies. I love going round to Frankie's house. For starters, her parents are really cool and friendly and speak to you like you're grown-up and not just some school kid. Plus she's got no horrid brothers or sisters (well, not yet, anyway – her mum's having a baby in a month or two actually) so she has a bedroom all to herself. *Plus* 'cos she's an only child, she has everything a kid could possibly want – a computer, loads of games, a telly in her bedroom... She is seriously kitted out, that girl.

When I went round there that night, it was all a bit different, though. Like I said, Frankie's mum is nearly eight months pregnant and apparently her blood pressure has gone dead high (that's how fast your heart pumps blood round the body, by the way – and if it gets too fast or too slow, you're in trouble, Dad says). So she's not working at the moment and Frankie's been a bit worried about her.

Maybe it was partly my fault that everything

46

had gone a bit strange there. You see, I'd asked Dad if he could help Frankie's mum at all, with him being a doctor and that.

"No," he'd said. "There's nothing I can prescribe for her – she'll just have to relax and take it easy." Then he pushed his glasses up his nose thoughtfully. "Maybe your friend Frankie could do a bit more around the house to help out – I'm sure that will be good for both of them!"

Typical parent remark, so I was kind of expecting Frankie to ignore it when I told her. "Help out around the house?" she'd said at the time. "Right." And I'd thought that would be the end of it. I wasn't expecting Frankie to turn into a housemaid!

Usually when I go round to her house, me and Frankie go straight up to her room and get stuck into some Playstation games. Or, if it's summer, we go out and mess about in the garden, or take our bikes out, or... Have fun, basically.

This night, though, we went straight into the kitchen. Now, I don't know about you, but

I tend to leave the kitchen area to parents. The only time I go in there is to make myself one of my hunger-buster sandwiches or to sneak some biscuits out of the tin while Mum's not looking. If I'm really unlucky, I'll be in there to wash up if I'm trying to get in Mum and Dad's good books. But that's about my limit!

This time though, Frankie was straight in there, apron on, filling the kettle with water and emptying the dishwasher. I hovered in the doorway, wondering what she was up to.

"Camomile tea, Mum?" Frankie called through to the living room where her mum was lying on the sofa.

She caught me looking at her with my gob hanging right open, and wiped her hands briskly on the apron. "It's relaxing," she told me. "Good for her."

"Frankie, you're acting like someone's aunt," I told her. "Shall we go and play Tomb Raider or something?"

"I'll just sort Mum out first," she said, like an old mother hen. She got out a tray and put this cup of yucky-smelling camomile tea and a banana on it, then frowned at the heating switch on the wall. "It's a bit cold in here," she sniffed.

"Frankie, it's boiling!" I said in disbelief. "What are you on about?"

"I don't want Mum getting cold," she said. "Kenny, don't look at me like that! I'm just trying to help her, that's all."

"Help her boil alive, you mean!" I snorted, pulling off my school jumper.

Just then, Mrs Thomas came waddling into the kitchen. I'm not being rude about her – Frankie's mum is ace – but you know how ginormous pregnant women get? They just start looking like ducks waddling around, if you ask me!

"Mum! What are you doing up?" Frankie said, and grabbed the tray off the table. I think she was about to give it to her, but you know how clumsy Frankie can be if she gets in a flap. Suddenly – *whooosh!* She'd stumbled on something, and hot stinky tea went splashing everywhere!

Mrs Thomas flopped weakly into a chair.

"Oh, Mum, I'm sorry!" Frankie wailed, rushing to the sink to get a cloth. "My foot skidded, and I..."

"What's going on in here?" came a voice. It was Frankie's dad, standing in the doorway.

"Frankie's 'helping' again," Mrs Thomas said to him. The two of them exchanged this weary, eye-rolling sort of look. I got the feeling they were both getting a bit sick of poor Frankie's help.

"Come on, Frankie, let's go and play upstairs," I said quickly.

"But I was going to cook dinner," Frankie began.

"No, you two go upstairs," said Frankie's mum. "I'm not totally useless yet, you know!"

"But..." Frankie started objecting, but her dad ushered us out of the kitchen.

"I was only trying to help!" she shouted as we went upstairs.

Honestly – parents. You can't win, can you?

CHAPTER FIVE

I've got to admit, I was a bit freaked out by Frankie's odd behaviour. It was like there was some other girl dressed up as Frankie, she was acting so out of character. Frankie is usually fun, fun, fun – not fuss, fuss, fuss. We leave all the fussing to Fliss! So as soon as we got to Brownies that night, I gathered the rest of the Sleepover lot together when Frankie was talking to Brown Owl about something.

"Emergency cheer-up sleepover required for Francesca Thomas," I said urgently. "She needs some laughs, badly! Look at her – she's

51

gone all stressed out about her mum!"

"Dr McKenzie prescribes again," Fliss teased.

"Yeah, too right," I said. "I'm prescribing her a sleepover tomorrow night with lots of sweets and stupid games – what do you reckon?"

"Let's do it," Lyndz agreed. "We could have it at my house, if you want. We haven't had one there for ages. I'll check with Mum tonight if it's OK."

"Cool!" I said, turning a cartwheel. "And we all have to bring lots of exciting ideas for things we can do to cheer Frankie up."

"No prizes for guessing what yours will be," Rosie groaned. "Or are you into something else today?"

"No, still got a one-track mind," I said cheerily – and then I suddenly remembered the indoor snowboarding centre again. Maybe what Frankie really needed was a day away from home, having fun on the slopes. YES! What a fantastic idea. Oh, who was I trying to kid? *I* needed it too! BADLY!

* * *

Sleepovers are always good at Lyndz's house. I mean, they're ace everywhere but somehow they seem to be especially ace at Lyndz's house. This is why:

Lyndz's mum has the wickedest dressing-up clothes in the world so we get to play lots of cool games in them.

We take Lyndz's bed down and all sleep on the floor in a line in our sleeping bags.

There's always lots of yummy food – and big portions too, 'cos Lyndz has got four brothers.

Lyndz's dog Buster usually sleeps in with us and joins in all our games.

Her mum and dad let us stay up really really late (as long as we don't wake up the baby...).

Sleepovers are just the best bit of the week. For a start, they're often on Fridays so it's the beginning of the weekend. No school – YEEEAHH! And even better – this week I had some megadocious news to tell everyone. After tons of begging and please-ing and promises to do lots of chores (yeah, right!), I'd talked my parents into.... Oh, well I won't say it now. You'll have to wait and see, like the others did!

It's so hard keeping your mouth shut when you've got a secret though, isn't it? I'm the worst person in the world – I always manage to blab it out, I just can't wait! But this time, I really tried to save it for the sleepover. I wanted to spring it on everyone as a surprise.

Lyndz's mum picked us up from school at three-thirty. "Hello, girls!" she said warmly as we ran out of the school gates. "Looking forward to the weekend?"

"Yeah!" we all shouted, squeezing into the car.

Sleepovers are always different, but usually the first thing we do is change out of our yucky school uniforms and play a few rounds of International Gladiators to work up an appetite for the sweets. This week, as soon as we were all in our jeans and T-shirts, Lyndz picked up a sleeping bag.

"Squishy-poo fighting first," she announced. "We haven't played that for ages!"

What did you say? You don't know what

squishy-poo fights are all about? It's one of our favourite things – even Fliss loves it! What you do is, you stuff your sleeping bags full of clothes and pillows so they are like giant, long, squishy cushions, and then you whack each other with them. Anyone falling over is out – and the winner is the last one on their feet! The problem is, you get so giggly doing it, it makes you get all weak – and before you know it, you've fallen in a heap!

We all raced to fill our squishy-poos. The rule is, as soon as you've stuffed your sleeping bag, you're allowed to start whacking.

"Aaargh!"

"Ooof!"

"Squishy-poo to you, too!"

In the end, it was just me and Rosie left, whacking away between fits of giggles. And then – doink! Rosie got me so hard on my left side that it winded me completely and I crashed on to the floor. "Mercy!" I gasped.

"I am the champion!" yelled Rosie, jumping up and down and waving her squishy-poo around.

I had a quick look at Frankie, who was acting a bit quiet. Still worrying about her mum, I guessed. "Let's play Zombie next," I suggested – one of Frankie's favourite games. "It's a dark and spooky night, and there's a Zombie on the prowl..."

"Good idea," said Lyndz, jumping up and drawing the curtains.

"Oh, no," said Fliss with a shudder. "Do we have to?"

"Oh yes," I said. "Ibble, obble, black bobble, ibble, obble, out!" I counted round everyone's fists. "Frankie, you're the Zombie!"

She gave a blood-curdling growl. "I'll give you five minutes!" she warned and left the room.

Lyndz switched the light off and Fliss gave a whimper. You're meant to play Zombie in a whole house 'cos you need lots of hiding places, but Lyndz's room is just about big enough. We all scurried about in the dark, trying to find somewhere to hide from the Zombie. I squashed myself under Lyndz's desk – I had no idea where the others had got to.

It had suddenly gone very quiet...

"Time's up! The Zombie is on the prowl!" Frankie called in a spooky voice. And then – *crrreeeeak!* She pushed the door open slowly and did a Zombie shuffle into the room. "Zombie... zombie... zombie..." she moaned hoarsely, feeling her way around the room.

I felt my skin prickling. Even though I knew it was only Frankie, I was still going all tingly and scared.

"I'm coming to get you," she whispered, and I shivered as I tried to work out where she was.

"Zombie... zombie... zombie..." she groaned in this creepy voice. Then there was a squawk from Lyndz. Caught! Now there were two Zombies!

"Zombie... zombie... zombie..." the pair of them moaned. I could feel my arms go all goosepimply as they shuffled closer. It's such a scary game!!

I scrunched myself up tight under the desk as I heard Frankie go past. Then, as Lyndz followed, I couldn't resist it – I shot an arm out and grabbed her ankle!

"*AAAAAAAAARGH!*" she screamed, completely freaked out. "Who was that?"

"It's the Zombie-eater!" I boomed – and then *everyone* started screaming!

Fliss ran over and put the light on. "I hate that game!" she said.

"We hadn't even finished it!" Rosie complained. "I had a wicked hiding place, as well."

There was a knock at the door, and Fliss nearly jumped out of her skin.

"It's only me," said Lyndz's mum, opening the door. "It sounds like there are some scary things happening in Lyndsey's bedroom – you might need a treat to calm yourselves down!"

She handed Fliss a box of Magnums and winked.

Fliss smiled weakly at her. "Thank you, Mrs Collins," she said, sounding relieved.

It wasn't until I'd taken a huge bite of Magnum that I remembered. I'd been so distracted by all the squishy-pooing and zombie-ing, I'd forgotten all about my amazing secret surprise.

I choked on my mouthful, trying to swallow it as fast as I could. "Hey, I've got something to tell you," I said excitedly, through a chunk of ice cream. "Guess WHAT?"

"You're entering the World Talking While Eating Championships?" Rosie suggested.

"You've decided never ever to scare me again?" Lyndz tried. "I hope?"

"No, I know," Fliss moaned. "You want us to run away to Switzerland together or something. I can tell by your face."

"Wrong, wrong and wrong," I said, smugly. "Although Fliss is kind of on the right track."

"I knew it!" she groaned.

"We don't have to run away to Switzerland to go snowboarding though," I said triumphantly. "There's an indoor skiing and snowboarding centre in Tolbury – only about half an hour away in the car. Emma told me. How about us all going there for a day's snowboarding?"

I was practically bursting with excitement.

"Well? What do you think? Mum and Dad have agreed to take us and everything!"

"Wow!" said Lyndz. "Really?"

"It sounds a bit dangerous to me," Fliss said, nibbling daintily at her Magnum. "I don't know if my mum would let me."

"It's not dangerous – you have a lesson and they teach you how to do it!" I said. "Honestly, Fliss, you're with an instructor all the time!"

She pursed her lips up and I could see she wasn't convinced. "You'd be good, anyway," I said to her. "What are you worried about? You're really good at sport!"

OK, so I was buttering her up a bit. But Fliss isn't bad at sport – she's quite OK at running and things like that, so it wasn't totally false of me. All right, so snowboarding was a bit different – so what?

"Do you think so?" she said, sounding pleased. "Really?"

"Yeah!" I said. "And you can ride a bike, can't you? So you must have good balance!"

"I suppose so," she said. Then she went a bit pink. "And I do like those fleecy tops they wear – I saw a thing about it in one of Andy's magazines..."

Good old Fliss! You can always count on her to say yes to something if it means an excuse to go shopping for a new outfit!

"What about the rest of you?" I said. One down, three to go...

"It sounds wicked!" said Lyndz. "Is it real snow?"

"Yeah, it is!" I said, grinning. "Real, white, wet, slippery snow! They make it with these mega snow-machines."

"Cool!" she said. "When you kept going on about it, I thought it was going to be something you could only do abroad – but if you can do it here... sounds brilliant!"

Two down...

"Rosie, what about you?" I asked.

Uh-oh. Rosie wasn't looking so easy to convince.

"How much is it going to cost?" she said cautiously. "Only it's coming up to Christmas and I don't know if Mum's got much cash to spare right now."

"It's not that much," I said quickly. "I'm sure you could ask for it as part of your Christmas present anyway – that would save her going shopping for it, wouldn't it?"

"I'll see what she says," she said, but I could tell she was feeling as excited as Lyndz underneath. "But hopefully yeah, count me in too! Sleepover Club on the slopes!"

"What do you reckon, Frankie?" I said anxiously. Frankie was the only one who hadn't said anything yet. "Won't be a proper Sleepover thing without you..."

She pulled a bit of a face. "It sounds ace and normally I'd go like a shot, but I don't know whether I can leave Mum at the moment."

I thought back to the way Frankie's mum had rolled her eyes about Frankie's 'helping'. Somehow I didn't think Frankie's mum would have a problem with Frankie going at all!

"She might like having the house to herself for the day," I said, trying to be tactful about it. "Give her a chance to really relax in peace."

"Maybe," said Frankie. "I'll ask."

I jumped in the air. "Whoopeeee!" I said.

"We're off! We can have a sleepover at ours on a Friday night and then go on the Saturday! It's just gonna be *sooo* excellent!"

"Even better – we can really rub it in with the M&Ms next week," Lyndz said with a wicked giggle. "They'll be sick as anything!"

"They'll hate us for it!" Fliss said, beaming broadly. "I can't wait to see their faces! We're going snowboarding, we're going snowboarding!"

Frankie leapt to her feet and pretended to snowboard along Lyndz's bedroom floor. "Look out, everyone – here I come!" she yelled. *"Neeeyyyooooowww!"*

I grinned to myself. My best mate bouncing around like a nutter again was the best thing I'd seen in ages!

CHAPTER SIX

The whole of the next week was just unbearable. Like I said, I hate having to wait for anything – and this time it practically *killed* me! First of all, before we could all get really excited about going, the others had to check with their parents that it was OK for them all to come. Lyndz's parents said yes right away. Then Rosie's. Fliss's mum was a bit worried about the whole thing, so I had to get my mum to phone her and reassure her that everything was going to be OK and her precious daughter wasn't about to break her neck on the slopes.

Then Frankie rang. "Hi!" I said. "What did your parents say about the snowboarding trip?"

There was this awful silence. "Well," she started – and then stopped.

"*What?*" I practically screamed down the phone. "Won't they let you go?"

"Well, they said I could go..." she started hesitantly.

I gave a huge sigh of relief. "YEEEEAHHH!" I shouted. "Oh, thank goodness for that! I thought you were going to say you couldn't come!"

There was another silence.

"Frankie?" I prompted.

She sighed heavily down the phone. Uh-oh. This wasn't sounding good.

"What's up?" I asked. "What's the matter?"

"It's my mum," Frankie said slowly. "She's got a hospital check-up that day."

"And?" I asked. It was starting to sound worse by the second.

"And... I want to go with her," Frankie said. "So I'm not going to go snowboarding."

"What?!" I screeched. "Why do you have to go with her? What's wrong with her?"

"Well, it's just a regular check-up but her blood pressure's still too high and... you know, I just want to be there," she said.

My heart sank. "And she wants you to go with her, does she?" I asked.

Frankie hesitated. "Actually, she said she'd rather I went with you lot and had some fun, but..."

I pounced on her words. "You should then, if that's what she wants! You can't really do anything to help her at the hospital anyway, can you?"

Another pause. "Noooo, but..."

"Tell you what," I said, thinking quickly. "Come with us and you can have a great day out and take your mind off it all. And you can ring her on her mobile if you're worried, can't you?"

"Ye-e-e-es," Frankie said doubtfully, "but..."

"She'll feel happier knowing that you're enjoying yourself and not getting all worried," I said, pulling out all the stops to try and convince her. Then I played my trump card. "Besides, you hate hospitals – I know you do!"

She sighed. "Yeah, you're right," she said, kind of reluctantly.

"Yipppppeeeeee!" I yelled. "So you're gonna come with us, then?"

"Yeah," she said. "But only if I can ring her while we're there."

"I'll even give you 50p for the phone call if it makes you come with us!" I said, a big grin stretching across my face. "It wouldn't be the same without you!"

After that near-miss, there came another blow to the plan – and this one was far more seriously BAD. We were all sitting and having tea on Monday night, and Mum only went and asked Molly and Emma if they wanted to come too, didn't she?

I choked on a bit of potato and Dad had to bang me on the back. "Oh, Mum!" I protested in horror. Those two would just wreck everything, I knew it! "Can't it be just the Sleepover Club?"

Mum pushed her glasses up her nose. She has this real thing about families doing everything together, worse luck. Just because she gets on with the rest of her family, it doesn't mean *I* do!

"Fair's fair," she said (one of her favourite phrases). "I'm going to phone up the snow centre tomorrow so I need to know how many people to book the lesson for. And it's only fair that Emma and Molly can come too if you're going."

"But there won't be enough room in the car," I argued, desperately trying to think of reasons to stop them coming along.

"We can take both cars," Mum said calmly. "Emma? Molly? What do you think?"

"I've got a netball match on Saturday so I can't," Emma said. "And even if I could, I wouldn't want to spend my Saturday with a bunch of ten-year-olds, thanks all the same!"

I gave her a cold stare but secretly was pleased that she didn't want to come. Good! Now there was only Molly the Monster I had to worry about...

"I'd love to come!" she said, smirking at me in that horrible way of hers. "Can Carli come too?"

Worse and worse and WORSE! Molly is a monster and a half but Carli... Carli's practically in the M&M league of yuckiness! And when Molly and Carli are together, it's *really* bad news. Suddenly my heart seemed to have sunk right down into my trainers.

"Of course she can – as long as it's OK with her parents," Mum smiled. "Right, that's that settled then."

"Oh, Muuum!" I groaned, but she gave me one of her looks.

"You're very lucky to be going at all, Laura – and don't you forget it!" she said sharply. "Now eat your dinner!"

I knew when I was beaten. GUTTED!!!

Once I'd just about gotten over the shock that it was going to be the Sleepover Club on the slopes plus yucky Molly plus even yuckier Carli, the rest of the week dragged by agonisingly slowly. Why is that when you're on holiday or it's the weekend, time whizzes by dead fast, but when you're waiting for Christmas or your birthday – or a snowboarding trip – it goes reeeeeaalllly slow, as if all the clocks in the world have broken down?!

The only good thing about the week was winding up the M&Ms. Ahh, a speciality of mine, don'tcha know! I can never resist the urge to make those two SQUIRM!

At school on Thursday morning, I broke the news to the others that my mum had booked us all in for a snowboarding lesson on the Saturday coming.

"Yahoo!" Lyndz said excitedly. "We're really going!"

"Hooray!" shouted Rosie.

We all jumped around cheering and yelling, even Frankie. Even Fliss!!

"What? Going where?" I heard two familiar nosey voices ask. AHA! The M&Ms had been eavesdropping!

"Maybe they're going back to Mars, where they belong," sniggered Emily.

"Hope so," Emily agreed. "Good riddance, wherever you're going! Don't hurry back, will you?"

"I'd never hurry anywhere to see you," I sneered back at her. "Don't flatter yourself, *darlin'*!"

"It's none of your business where we're going, anyway," Frankie said, her nose in the air. "Although it's going to be great getting away from you two for a while!"

"Can't wait," Rosie said. "No smelly Ems around, polluting the air..."

"Just clean, fresh snow," Lyndz said teasingly.

That got their curiosity going! "Snow?" Emily said. "Who said it's going to snow? It's not cold enough yet!"

"Where we're going there's always snow," Fliss said smugly. "So poo to you!"

I snorted with laughter. Fliss thinks "poo" is the rudest word in the world! "Well said," I agreed. "Double poo to you with a cherry on top!"

"And a cocktail umbrella!" Frankie chuckled.

71

"And a snowboard sticking out of the top!" Lyndz spluttered, between giggles.

"Snowboarding! Is that what you're doing?" Emma said, disbelievingly.

"Yeah," I gloated. "Jealous by any chance, are we?"

"I can't wait to go snowboarding, can you?" Rosie said to the rest of us. "It sounds so wicked!"

"So exciting," said Frankie solemnly.

"What, you mean you've never been?" Fliss said to the M&Ms sorrowfully. "Never mind – we'll tell you all about it next week!"

Do you know – for once, we had the M&Ms well and truly speechless. It was *ace*. They just couldn't think of any comeback! They both stood there, looking red-faced and totally jealous, and then in the end, Emily growled, "Hope you break your necks!" and they both stomped off in a huff.

We all collapsed into laughter. Definitely one–nil to the Sleepover Club!

At long last, Friday finally rolled around and

we all charged back from school for the sleepover at my house. Sleepovers are a bit tricky at my house because of me and Molly sharing a room. Molly usually sulks if she has to move into Emma's for the night, and makes a big fuss about letting my friends sleep on her precious half of the room. Like we're really going to trash the place! Us!

This week we had a bit of a result though, as she went to stay with Carli for the night. YES!!! Mum was going to pick them up on the way to the snow centre. So I suppose something good had come out of Molly going snowboarding with us – just about…

The first thing we did at Friday's sleepover was make an assault course in my bedroom. The only good-ish thing about sharing with Molly is it means we have a fairly big room between us – plus there are two beds which are good for playing trampolines on!

The assault course went like this. Three big bounces on my bed and a leap off, then a forward roll over to Molly's bed. Then we had to get on the floor and swarm under Molly's bed (past the smelly trainers, poo! That was an assault course in itself!) then cartwheel over to the bedroom door. Finally, a wriggle under our big saggy beanbag, a jump up to the windowsill, crawl along it and jump from there back on to my bed. Phew! What a brilliant course!

The only problem was the cartwheels. We were all going round in turn, but somehow Lyndz managed to kick Rosie in the face and then we all got a bit bunched up and kept bumping into each other. Excellent fun, though!

When we'd gone round a few times, I jumped up. "I know!" I said. "I'll teach you a few snowboarding tricks that Nick showed me."

"Ooh, Nick!" said Rosie at once.

"Nick says..." giggled Frankie.

"Nick knows *everything*!" said Fliss, clasping her hands to her chest and looking all dreamy and pathetic.

"Very funny," I said sarkily. "Now, then, I'll tell you how to strap your feet to the— *aaaargh!!*"

"Know-all!" said Lyndz.

"Show off!" said Frankie.

I couldn't get any further because suddenly the others were all pelting me with pillows, school bags and Molly's teddy bear. Somehow we ended up having this huge throwing match, all screaming and giggling hysterically.

"Knickers to Nick!" Lyndz screeched. "Big baggy white knickers to Nick!"

"Big Dad's Y-fronts to Nick!" Rosie gurgled. "He's not going snowboarding tomorrow – and we are!"

CHAPTER SEVEN

I could hardly get to sleep that night, I was so excited. And then when I finally did get to sleep, I dreamed about skimming around corners, deep white snow, speeding down mountains. I guess you could say something was on my mind!

I was the first to wake up, as usual. Why is it that on a school day, Mum has to practically drag me out of bed, but on a Saturday, my eyes ping open about six in the morning and I'm ready to go-go-GO!?

I lay in my sleeping bag, listening to the

others breathing, and I hugged myself tight with excitement. My tummy felt like it was fizzing up as I lay there, grinning away to myself like an idiot! HOOOORAY!! It was Saturday! We were going!!!

Mum was being super-nice that morning, and when we all came down for breakfast, she put plates of bacon, egg, mushrooms and fried bread in front of us. "It's a snowboarder's breakfast," she told us with a wink. "Need to build your strength up, don't you?"

"Definitely," I said, through a mouthful of eggy toast. "Thanks, Mum!"

Once we'd eaten our snowboarders' breakfasts, we piled into the cars. As Fliss, Lyndz and Rosie all got into my mum's car, I glumly agreed to go in the other car with Molly and Carli and my dad.

"I'd better keep you company, then," Frankie said, climbing in next to me. "Can't leave you to face the monsters on your own, can I?"

"Thanks," I said, sighing. "You're a true friend, Frankie Thomas!"

On the way to Carli's house, Dad made the

mistake of asking Frankie how her mum was. Instantly Frankie got her worried face on all over again.

"I didn't really like leaving her today," she confessed. "She's got her hospital check-up – and then, even worse, her and my dad were talking about going shopping! I mean, the stress of going into Leicester will send her blood pressure right up again, don't you think? She'll be on her feet all day – and there'll be all those people bumping into her..."

Frankie looked out the window as we sped along the road. "Maybe I should have stayed with her," she said softly.

"Don't be daft!" I said in alarm. Frankie looked like she was about to change her mind about coming with us – which would be AWFUL!

"She'll be fine, pet," Dad said gruffly. I think he's got a soft spot for Frankie, even if he does call her "Mad Frankie Thomas" sometimes. "The doctor will tell her if she's not fit to do anything strenuous, I'm sure. And just think, if she does go out, and has a really awful day shopping, at least it'll put her off going again for a good while, eh?"

"That's true," I said quickly. "And we're gonna give her a ring from the snow centre to check she's OK, yeah?"

"Yeah," Frankie agreed. "I'm probably worrying about nothing."

Phew – that was a close one! I found myself breathing out so heavily, I steamed the window right up.

It took us about half an hour to get there – and boy, was I glad to get out! Molly sat in the front with Dad, which meant that Creepy Carli sat in the back with me and Frankie. Triple YUCK. I'm not joking – nearly all the way there, she was digging her elbow into me. You know me – just can't ignore anyone if I think they're trying to have a pop at me, so after a bit, I was digging my own elbow into her, just as hard. Next thing you know, we're having an elbow fight on the back seat, and Dad has to pull over and shout at us to stop scrapping.

Why does Molly have to have such a HORRIBLE best friend?!

I was just thinking up plans to bury Molly and Carli in deep, deep snow, when Frankie nudged me. "Look – that must be it!" she said excitedly, pointing to a big white building in the distance.

The snow centre – COOL!!!

"Wow!" I breathed, unable to take my eyes off it. I felt like I was about to burst!

It was about eleven o'clock when we got there, so we had an hour to kill before our lesson at twelve. We met up with Mum and the others in the car park. I started jumping up and down, partly with excitement and partly 'cos it was so cold.

"Right, girls," Mum said. "Me and your dad are going to go to the gym for an hour while you have your lesson, OK? Then we'll meet up with you and we can all go for a swim. Then we can have a late lunch before coming home. What do you think of that?"

"Perfect!" I said. "Can we go in now? It's freezing!"

Dad laughed. "I really don't think the

snowboarding area is going to be any warmer, do you?" he said.

Mum and Dad took us round the complex so we knew exactly where everything was. We finished up in the spectators' gallery.

"Look," Frankie said with interest, "there's a snowboarding lesson going on!"

We all looked down eagerly. A row of people were wobbling about and falling all over the place.

"It looks a bit difficult," Fliss said uncertainly. "Do you think we'll be able to do it?"

"Oops! Over she goes!" Lyndz giggled, pointing to a large lady in a bright yellow puffa jacket who'd just toppled over into the snow.

"Look at him – right on his bum!" I said, laughing my head off at some poor bloke who was scrambling to his feet again.

"Ouch!" Mum said sympathetically. "Are you sure you still want to do this?"

"Definitely!" Molly said, eyes glued to the action below.

Fliss opened her mouth to say something.

"Yeah, of course we do!" I said quickly. "And anyone who doesn't dare is a CHICKEN!"

Fliss's mouth shut again, and I grinned to myself. I had her sussed!

"Hang on a minute – isn't that Nick?" sharp-eyed Rosie said, pointing to a guy in a blue woolly hat who was slithering about all over the snow.

I snorted. "I don't think so!" I said scornfully.

Lyndz scrunched up her eyes and peered in the direction of Rosie's finger. "Well, it looks like him," she said, slowly.

"Well, it isn't!" I said. "He can snowboard already – he's been snowboarding all round the world, he told me! Anyway, you've only seen him once, so what do you know?"

"I went into Mega Sports with Andy last week," Fliss chimed in. "And it does look like him, if you ask me!"

"Well, no-one *is* asking you, are they?" I said defensively. "And you lot think *I've* got him on the brain! Come on. We'd better go and get ready for our lesson."

*   *   *

Once we got into the boots-and-boards room, I found myself getting a bit bossy. Well, not bossy. Just... telling the others what to do, I suppose.

We went over to the junior boards section, and I pounced upon a turquoise board just like the one I'd stood on in the shop, although this one was about half the size! "Ah, Nick says this is a good make," I said, feeling grand. "It's the one I went on last time, actually."

"What – do you mean, when you just stood on it, in the shop?" Frankie said scathingly.

"Yeah, well, it's more than *you've* done," I pointed out. "And Nick said—"

"He didn't!" Rosie said sarcastically before I'd even had the chance to finish.

"What, Nick did?" Lyndz teased, joining in. "Your hero!"

"Nick really said that?" said Fliss. "You should have told us before!"

Honestly – you'd think they were jealous of my cool friend Nick or something! I couldn't help it if he was an experienced sporting hero, could I?

"Nick, Nick, Nick!" Frankie said suddenly. "It sounds to me like you'd rather be with him than with us!"

"Of course I wouldn't!" I said in astonishment. "I'd much rather be with you lot!"

"Good," she sniffed, not looking me in the eye. "Well, that's all right, then."

I was shocked. "Just 'cos I've been to see him a few times!" I said hotly. "It doesn't mean anything!"

Was Frankie jealous? I couldn't believe it!

"Oh, stop showing off in front of your friends," Molly said with a smirk, elbowing me out of the way. "Come on, Carls, let's get the best boots."

When Molly says things like that to me I really want to punch her one, but this time, I managed to hold my tongue all the time we were putting on our boots and collecting our boards. Then I held it a bit longer as we all trooped out in the snowy area where we'd be having our lesson.

Then I just couldn't hold it any more, and

picked up a *huge* handful of snow and stuffed it down Molly's neck. I'd give her showing off in front of my friends!

"*Aaaargh!*" she screeched as the freezing snow hit her bare skin. "You little..."

"Snow fight!" yelled Rosie in delight, and grabbed an armful of snow to hurl at Carli.

Suddenly we were all screaming with excitement and chucking snow about like anything. As it was five against two, Molly and Carli were getting soaked, fast!! I was starting to feel quite glad they'd come with us after all!

But then – *screeeeee!* A whistle blew, and we all jumped. I jumped so hard that I chucked my last snowball over my head and behind me.

"Girls, this is a snowboarding lesson, not a zoo!" came a sharp voice. "Stop that imme—"

Then there came this awful spluttering sound like someone trying to cough through snow...

We turned round in horror to see a tall woman in a fleecy red tracksuit wiping snow off her face. She glared at me as if I was a cockroach or something, and I suddenly had a very nasty feeling about where my last snowball had gone. WHOOPS!!!

"My name's Suzi and I'll be teaching you today," she said. "And I think you'd better all calm down before we do anything." She looked straight at me. "Now, is that clear?"

"Yes," I said in a small voice.

Her icy look seemed to thaw a bit, and then she gave us a smile. "Good," she said. "Let's get snowboarding!"

CHAPTER EIGHT

I hate to say it, but you know what? At first, I was just the *weeniest* bit disappointed by our snowboarding lesson. I know, I know – after all that fuss I made and everything. But in my head, I'd imagined us all on the main slope pretty much straightaway, cruising down dead fast, just like Nick had told me he'd done, and learning all these ace tricks.

Instead, we were on this baby slope – and even worse, Suzi told us there was no way we could go on the main slope until we'd had a few lessons and knew what we were doing.

Doh! So much for my big ideas, eh?

Suzi caught sight of my disappointed face and laughed. "Can you imagine if we just let anyone on the main slopes?" she said, shaking her head at the thought. "There would be all sorts of crashes and injuries – it would be very dangerous. Before you can go on, you have to prove you can control your speed, know how to stop and make turns properly. It's only fair on everyone else, don't you think?"

"Yeah," everyone said.

"I suppose so," I said grudgingly.

But I soon cheered up once the lesson got underway. It was such fun! And then I started to feel really glad we *weren't* on the main slopes, as one by one, we wobbled, fell down and knocked someone else over. It was really difficult – almost as tricky as skateboarding down the stairs had been!!

First of all, we had to get our boards securely fastened to our feet. It had been easy when Nick had done it all for me as I'd just stood there and let him do everything – but now it was down to us to do it ourselves.

"Make sure your board is facing *across* the hill," called Suzi, checking we were all in a good position. "We don't want you shooting off without being properly fastened in, do we? Now, put your front foot in while you're standing up. These boards have step-in bindings, so step the toe in first, and push the heel down until you hear a click. Got it?"

A series of clicks from along the line confirmed that we'd all managed it so far.

"Now put on your safety leash," Suzi said. "It goes on your front leg."

"What's it for?" asked Frankie.

"Well, if you fall over – which I'm pretty sure most of you will do – it stops the board from running away," Suzi explained. "OK. All ready?"

We were.

"Now, you always have to sit down to put your back foot in. Make sure there's no snow in the binding or on the bottom of your boot. Step the back foot in just like you did with the front." She waited until she'd heard all of our bindings click in place. "Now comes the fun part," she said with a grin. "Standing up!"

I bet you never thought standing up would be difficult, did you? You have to try this, then! Standing up when your feet are fastened to a bit of wood is reeeeallly tricky!! Take it from someone who knows.

"The main thing to remember is, always put the same weight on both feet," Suzi told us. "Have a go. If you get really stuck, roll over on to your knees and then stand up that way."

Well, one by one we just about managed to get up and stand there in a line on our boards. But then Lyndz started wobbling, made a grab for Rosie – and the pair of them collapsed down face first into the snow! I found myself giggling so much I thought I was going to go the same way and had to clutch at Frankie to keep myself vertical. This was going to be a lot harder than I'd thought!

Once we'd got used to standing up on the boards without wobbling off, we started going down the baby slope – or bunny slope, as Suzi called it. She pushed herself off and showed us how it was done – making it look like the easiest thing in the world, of course!

I went down next. WHHHEEEEEE! It was brilliant!! I stuck my arms out to the sides for balance, gritted my teeth and went down in a dead straight line, all the way to the bottom. As soon as I'd made it safely down, I promptly fell over on my bum. All the others cheered their heads off from the top.

"Way to go, girl!" yelled Frankie, punching the air.

She went next, and was just about to push herself off when Carli gave her a shove from behind…

"Wooooaaahhhhh!" Frankie shouted as she shot down the slope. She recovered her balance a bit, but was going so fast, she had to windmill her arms about to keep herself upright. "Heeeeeeelllllp!" she screamed as she wobbled over and then tumbled down the hill. *Bump!* She landed in a heap at the bottom.

"Are you OK?" I called, scrabbling to undo my bindings. I rushed over to her – and heard Molly and Carli sniggering from the top.

Frankie struggled to her feet. "I'm gonna get you for that!" she yelled to Carli. Then she rubbed her bum where she'd landed on it. "Ouch," she moaned. "This snow feels more like rock!"

Suzi rushed over. "All right there?" she asked. "You did very well, considering that blonde girl pushed you like that. If she does that again, she'll have to sit the lesson out."

She looked up at Carli with a frown. "You there," she shouted. "Let's have less of the pushing, or your lesson ends right here. Got that?"

Me and Frankie smirked at each other and pulled horrible faces at Carli behind Suzi's back. Always good to see the enemy getting a ticking off!

Fliss was next. She looked very nervous about the whole thing, and stood there for ages, fiddling about with her bindings as if they were going to pop undone any second.

"Come on! Give it a go!" Suzi called encouragingly.

Fliss looked warily over her shoulder to check Carli and Molly were out of pushing distance. Fliss hates people doing things like that. She either gets dead cross about it or bursts into tears. When she was sure she was safe, she stood up very stiff and straight and pushed herself off, arms rigidly out to the sides, as if she were made of wood.

"Very good," Suzi shouted as Fliss came down the slope. "Try and relax your body a bit!"

Fliss wasn't about to relax anything for fear of toppling over. She came all the way down in the same stiff way, coming neatly to a stop at the bottom. Only then did she allow her arms to relax. She had this tiny chuffed smile and her cheeks were flushed pink.

"That was very good," Suzi said warmly. "Your balance was excellent!"

Fliss went even pinker. "Thank you," she said, struggling to undo her feet from the board. Her eyes were shining. "That was fun!"

Soon we'd all been down a few times and were starting to get a feel for it. Suzi taught us how to come to a clean stop by digging our back foot right into the board and leaning all our weight on to it, and then taught us how to do left and right turns on the slope. It was just so much fun, whizzing down one by one – but then when Suzi told us that our time was almost up, I nearly cried. I couldn't believe the time had flown by so quickly!

"We'll have one more go each, and then that's about it for your first lesson," she said.

"Ohhhh!" I moaned. "Already?"

She smiled at me. "Afraid so. You've done very well though. I think you're a bit of a natural, Kenny!"

I glowed with pride. I was practically radioactive with glowing! A natural!! She thought I was a natural, after one lesson! How cool was that?!

I should have left it there, of course. I should have just accepted the compliment and left it at that. But no. That's not me, is it? Kenny McKenzie always has to go one further – as I was about to prove yet again!

CHAPTER NINE

OK, I admit it. I was showing off.

All right, all right – so I was showing off a lot.

I just couldn't resist it, OK?!

I was about to have my last go down the slope – and who could say when I'd get the chance to do this again? Maybe not for years!! Maybe this was the last time I'd get to snowboard until I was grown up, and that was just *ages* away.

The way I looked at it, it was my last chance to try something a bit... well, a bit adventurous. And there's no need to look at me like that. I bet you'd have done the same.

"Come on, then, Kenny," Suzi said. "Last go. Let's see you make a left turn first, followed by a right turn to finish off with."

"OK," I said.

Do you ever get a voice in your head that urges you to do naughty things? I seem to get it all the time. And this time it was a loud voice. This time it was saying, "Try one of those jumps that Nick told you about!"

The sensible side of me was trying to ignore the naughty voice – but this voice was just *sooooo* persuasive...

"Go on, Kenz," Frankie said. "What are you waiting for?"

"Ooh, Kenny's scared!" Carli mocked, and started making all these chicken noises at me.

Well, if there's one thing I'm not, it's a chicken. No-one could ever call me that!

"Right, Carli," I thought. "I'll show YOU!!!"

I had in mind this thing I'd seen on one of the videos in Nick's shop. I think it's called the corkscrew, but basically it's someone on a snowboard jumping up and whizzing round and round in the air and then landing flat and zooming off again. COOOL!

I was a natural, wasn't I? I reckoned I could have a go at it – and really impress Suzi!

"Watch this!" I said grandly.

I started off down the slope. Then, about a third of the way down, I bent my knees and tried to whizz myself round like I'd seen the guys on the video do. It had all looked so easy for them...

"Kenny, what are you...?" I heard Suzi call anxiously – but suddenly the world had become a blur. With a massive effort, I'd launched myself into the air, spun round and round – and landed flat on my back. YOWCH! I gave a scream as my ankle was wrenched from the snowboard and I rolled all the way down the rest of the slope, my board bumping along after me.

There was this terrible silence. All I could hear was the sound of my own pain roaring all over my body. Every part of me seemed to be throbbing and aching. I lay in a heap, breathing quickly, my heart pounding.

Suzi ran over. "Kenny, what on *earth* were you trying to do?" she shouted, sounding half-cross and half-frightened.

"I'm sorry," I gasped, as dizzy spells came and went in my head. For a second I thought I would faint. "I was trying to do the corkscrew," I said, feeling like an idiot.

"The *corkscrew*?! Kenny, you're a beginner, remember!" she said. "You can't expect to do that kind of trick for months!"

I groaned as she started taking the board off my other foot. "Ouch," I said. "Ow – *please* don't touch my ankle. It's really really sore!"

Frankie snowboarded down to us. "What's up?" she asked breathlessly. "Do you want me to get your dad, Kenz? He's a doctor," she added for Suzi's benefit.

"Yes, that's a good idea," Suzi said. "This ankle's had a nasty twist. It definitely needs some looking at."

Frankie took her board off and charged away. One by one, the others came down the slope and stood around us.

"You idiot, Kenny!" Molly said scornfully.

"It looked good, though," Lyndz said, trying to be kind. "It did look really good, Kenny."

"Yeah, till she went whack on her back!" Carli sniggered. "That just looked stupid, if you ask me!"

"I'm really sorry, Suzi," I said in a small voice.

"Well, it was a very silly thing to do, Kenny, but I've got to confess – I did exactly the same thing on my first lesson," Suzi said, winking at me. "We must be as bad as each other."

"Did you?" I asked, feeling a bit better.

"Yep," she said. "Broke my wrist. It was a good lesson to me, though. It taught me to know my limits."

"Well, this has taught me how painful an ankle can feel," I grumbled. "OW!!"

"Here's Dad," Molly called. "He doesn't look very happy, Kenny."

Dad was picking his way over the snow with the medical bag of tricks that he takes everywhere. "How did I know this was going to happen?" he said gruffly. "And how did I know it was going to happen to you?"

Mum was right behind. "Oh, love, are you all right?" she said sympathetically. "How did you manage that?"

Dad knelt down and took my boot and sock off. My ankle was about the size of a grapefruit and still throbbing.

"Ouch!" I yelled as he pressed it all over. "Careful, Dad!"

"It's not broken," he said at last. "But it's a nasty sprain. We'll have to get that strapped up for you."

Suzi got to her feet. "Well, I'm sorry the lesson had to end this way, everyone," she said. "But you all did very well, and I hope to see you again for another lesson soon. Bye!"

Dad snorted as she walked over to the next group of people. "Not if I've got anything to do with it!" he said. "I don't want my daughters to be crocked before they're even in their teens!"

So that was me out of action for the rest of the day. I couldn't believe that my daredevil ways had got me in trouble AGAIN! That's the last time I do anything like that, I'm telling you.

Well. Until I forget and do it next time, of course...

Dad strapped my ankle up tightly and helped me hobble along. I suddenly felt really tired after all the excitement.

"That was so excellent," Rosie said, skipping along to the pool changing rooms.

"Awesome," Frankie agreed happily, her eyes shining. "I loved doing those turns, didn't you?"

"We'll definitely have to try and come again," Lyndz said. "I want to have a go at the corkscrew too!"

"No, you don't," I said feelingly, wincing with pain as I hobbled along.

"Thanks ever so much for taking us," said Fliss to my mum and dad, going a bit pink. "We did really enjoy it."

"Glad to hear it, Felicity," Mum said, sounding pleased. "Do you think you lot have got enough energy for a swim next?"

"YEEEEAAAHHH!" everyone shouted. Well, everyone except me – old Hop-Along!

I turned to Frankie. "Do you want to give

your mum a ring first?" I asked. "I might as well come with you, seeing as I won't be swimming!"

"Yeah, good idea," she said. "Don't wait for us, everyone – I'll catch up with you all in the changing rooms!"

The two of us slowly made our way to the telephone area, Frankie helping me hobble along. I sat and waited while she spoke to her mum.

When she came off the phone, she looked a thousand times happier. "Oh, guess what! Her blood pressure's getting back to normal – and everything's fine with the baby!"

"Oh, brilliant!" I said, giving her a hug. "That's ace news. Do you feel better?"

"Yeah, tons better," she said, grinning all over her face. "I've just been so looking forward to having a little brother or sister. I wanted it all to be perfect, you know what I mean? I've just been so worried about her – and now it looks like it's all going to be fine. Brilliant!"

"Yeah," I said – and then I paused,

remembering what she'd said to me earlier. "Frankie, did you mean what you said before, about me caring more about Nick than the Sleepover Club?"

She looked a bit sheepish. "Not really," she said. "I was just in a bit of a funny mood."

"Really?" I said.

She nodded. "Really."

"So we're best mates again?" I asked. Well, I had to check, didn't I?

She smiled at me, and helped me to my feet. "Definitely best mates again."

While the others were all swimming and having a good time in the pool, I had to sit in the spectators' area with Mum and Dad. Typical of my luck, eh?! I was really starting to regret being a daredevil – as usual. The only good bit was watching the others grabbing Carli and dunking her in the deep end. I was just gutted I wasn't there to help them!

After they'd all got showered and changed again, we had a quick lunch and then it was time to go home again.

"How's it going, Hop-Along?" Frankie asked me as we headed for reception and the way out.

"Oh, it's OK," I said. "Better to twist your ankle snowboarding than running for a bus, I suppose. At least everyone's going to ask me how I did it, and I can tell them all about today!"

"Oh yes, I did it snowboarding, don't you know?" Rosie said, putting on a posh voice. "What? You've never been? Oh, darling, you're missing out!"

"Yeah, and I can't wait to tell Nick about it all," I said enthusiastically. "I feel like I'll know what he's talking about now – I'll feel like a *real* snowboarder, if you know what I mean."

"Talk of the devil..." Lyndz said, pointing straight ahead. "Why not tell him right now?"

I blinked in surprise. There at the reception desk was... was Nick!!

CHAPTER TEN

I could hardly believe my eyes. Nick! In the flesh! So had it really been him slithering around on the beginner slopes? No... it just *couldn't* have been! He was far too experienced for that! What about all those resorts he said he'd been to? What about everything he'd said to me?

"It must be a massive coincidence," I said in the end, with a frown. "Maybe he's come here to teach a lesson or something."

The others exchanged looks, and Frankie raised one of her eyebrows in disbelief.

I started to feel a bit weird about the whole thing. Just what *was* he doing here, anyway?

We were almost level with him now, and I was just about to tap him on the shoulder when he reached the front of the queue at the reception desk.

"Hi. Could I book another Beginners' lesson for next week, please?" he said. "Yeah, it's Nick Parker..."

I nearly fell over in shock. *Beginners'* lesson? What?? What was going on?

"Did you hear that?" Frankie said. "He's a beginner too!" She burst out laughing. "After all that!"

The others all started to giggle. "What a liar!" Fliss said indignantly. "Pretending he knew all about it!"

Nick obviously heard her because he turned round quickly. When he saw the five of us staring at him accusingly, he flushed a deep red.

"Hi, Kelly," he said weakly. "Fancy seeing you here."

"It's *Kenny*," I said, feeling scornful. "And fancy seeing *you* here – booking a Beginners' lesson!"

He went even redder, right up to the roots of his hair. It looked like a beetroot had been plopped on top of his neck instead of a head. "Well, er... I've got a trip to France planned soon," he said falteringly. "Just brushing up on a few tricks, you know..."

"Oh yeah?" Frankie said disbelievingly, putting her hands on her hips. "You made out to Kenny you were an expert!"

"Well, I..." he said, obviously trying to think of something to say.

The woman at the reception desk tapped her pen loudly. "Excuse me, sir – your ticket?"

Nick grabbed it, looking grateful for the excuse to finish the conversation. "Thanks," he said to her. "Well, you guys, gotta go," he said, not meeting any of us in the eye.

"Yeah, I bet you have," Rosie said loudly.

"What a creep!" Frankie said as he scurried off to the car park.

"And what a liar, coming out with all those

stories!" Fliss said, folding her arms across her chest.

I said nothing. I just couldn't believe that my hero had turned out to be so... so *pathetic*. He was no more experienced at snowboarding than us!

Lyndz slipped an arm in mine. "I bet he's never even *tried* a corkscrew," she said comfortingly. "You're far more daring than him!"

"Yeah! All he can do is work in a shop and make stories up about it," Frankie said. "Sad!!"

"Sad, but quite funny as well," Rosie said. "Did you see his face? He was so gutted!! He's probably terrified you're going to spoil his cool image in the shop now!"

"You should do," Lyndz said. "It would serve him right!"

I knew they were trying to cheer me up but I couldn't help feeling massively disappointed in Nick. I'd built him up in my head to be this total super-cool dude, the kind of person that I really wanted to be. He'd been my role model, coming out with all those stories about the amazing things he'd done all over the world. And then to find out that really he was just a bit sad, as Frankie said... It had made me feel all mixed up. How could I have fallen for all his stories like that?

I felt dead quiet and confused. What a let down!

"Who cares about him, anyway?" Fliss said. "We're proper snowboarders ourselves now. We've got our own stories to tell!"

"Yeah," Frankie said. "And you've even got an injury to show off about, Kenz."

"That's true," I said.

"And you're a natural, remember," Lyndz pointed out. "You'll probably be giving HIM lessons soon!"

"Yeah," I said, brightening up. "That would show him, wouldn't it?"

Then I remembered how this had been a one-off treat that I'd had to beg and plead for. "Mind you, when will we ever get to go again?" I groaned.

"There's always birthdays," Frankie said. "And Christmas coming up..."

"And our parents are soooo generous, they're bound to take us again soon," Molly said, winking at Dad. "Aren't they?"

He laughed. "We'll see," was all he would say.

"Goodbye, snow centre," I said sadly as we got near the exit doors. "Hope to see you again soon, hint hint..."

Then Molly pushed open one of the doors, and we all gasped...

It was snowing outside! Real snow – and lots of it!

Frankie was the first to react. "You know what this means, don't you?" she said, grabbing me excitedly. "Sledging in the park! Almost as good as snowboarding!"

"And it's free!" Lyndz yelled, jumping up and down. "Yippeeee!"

Well, what do you know? Things were looking up already. "I can practise doing the corkscrew on a sledge," I said excitedly, imagining in my head how totally cool it would look.

"Oh, no you don't," Mum said warningly.

"Not until that ankle's better, anyway!"

"We can have a snowball fight with the M&Ms!" Rosie said gleefully.

"We can build snowmen!" Fliss squealed.

"Sledging races down Cuddington Hill!" Lyndz shouted, jumping up and down.

Suddenly the world seemed a much better place as the snowflakes drifted down into our hair. Even Carli and Molly were dancing about in it.

I stuck my tongue out to catch a snowflake. "Yum!" I said as it melted in my mouth.

"You have to make a wish now," Mum said, with a smile. "I wonder what it's going to be?"

I screwed my eyes up tight and crossed all my fingers. Guess what I wished for?!

Well, that's about it from me on our snowboarding story. I'll tell you what, though. When my ankle's better and we sort out another trip, you'll have to come with us. Honestly – it's just the best!! And next time, I'm determined to work out how to do the corkscrew properly, too...

But guess what? In the meantime, I'm boycotting Mega Sports and going back to the old sports shop in Leicester again. Maybe I'll find a new role model there, who knows?

Hang on – the phone's ringing. Just a sec...

"Hi, Kenz – it's Frankie. Just to say that now Mum's OK again, I've been thinking about some more brilliant things the Sleepover Club can do together, and I was wondering if you fancied coming over so we can make some plans together..."

What do you reckon? Of course I fancied it! Now *that's* what I call a happy ending!

Well, looks like that's all from me this time. I'd better go. I said I'd meet her in half an hour. See ya later, alligator!